Whispers from The Sta Secrets

Jan Miller

ISBN: 978-1-963919-73-8

Dedication

This book is dedicated to parents.

John and Shirley, my brother Phillip, and my sister Letitia.

Special thanks to Nate Fox.

Acknowledgment

I would like to express my deepest gratitude to my publisher (Bane Thompson), whose belief in me from the very beginning has made this journey possible.

To my wonderful and loving family, your unwavering support and example of what a family should be are my constant source of strength and inspiration.

I also extend heartfelt thanks to my friends around the world, whose love and encouragement have been with me every step of the way, regardless of the path I take.

Thank you all.

Table of Contents

About the Author

This book is a heartfelt tribute to the most important people in my life—my children and my husband. It is inspired by my sons, Daniel and Austyn, and my beautiful daughter, Heathyr. Each of them has been a source of endless joy and strength, guiding me through both the triumphs and the challenges of life. Their love and support have been the bedrock of my inspiration, fueling my desire to share this message with the world.

Equally significant is the support and encouragement from my husband, Jim. His constant reassurance and belief in my abilities have been a driving force behind this book. Jim's steadfast confidence in me is a reminder that there are no limits to what we can achieve when we have the support of those we love.

In life, we inevitably face trials and obstacles. This book is a testament to the resilience of the human spirit and a reminder that, despite the challenges we encounter, our faith can remain unshaken. It serves as a call to hold steadfast to our beliefs and to cherish and fight for the bonds of family.

My hope is that readers will find solace and inspiration in these pages, recognizing that even in the face of adversity, the strength of faith and the support of loved ones is invaluable. May this book encourage you to embrace your journey with courage and conviction, knowing that you are never alone in your struggles.

Chapter 1: Shadows of the Past

The cold, metallic clang of the train station's gate echoed through the empty lot, sending shivers down Claire Kensington's spine. She stood still, staring at the dilapidated structure before her, its once majestic facade now a crumbling testament to forgotten times. The air around her seemed to thicken with the weight of memories she had long tried to bury.

Her fingers trembled slightly as she fished the keys from her purse, the government's official seal glinting ominously under the weak afternoon sun. The moment the letter arrived, she knew she had to come here. The offer was too enticing to pass up, but it was the station's shadowy past that truly beckoned her—a past intertwined with her own in ways she wished she could forget.

Claire inhaled deeply, steeling herself before pushing open the heavy gate. The rusted hinges protested loudly, a mournful cry that reverberated through the cavernous space beyond. Dust motes danced in the thin streams of light piercing through the cracked windows, casting eerie patterns on the floor. She took a cautious step inside, her heels clicking against the stone, each sound magnified in the vast emptiness.

The silence was oppressive, broken only by the distant hum of the city outside and the occasional skittering of unseen critters. She paused, listening, half-expecting to hear the echo of her grandfather's laughter, a sound she hadn't heard in decades. But only silence greeted her.

Claire's gaze swept over the graffiti-scarred walls, the shattered remnants of ticket booths, and the rotting benches. Her grandfather had been found here, his life brutally ended without a trace of the killer or a hint of motive. The case had gone cold, leaving a void that had gnawed at her ever since.

As she ventured deeper into the station, a sense of unease settled over her. She couldn't shake the feeling of being watched, of unseen eyes tracking her every move. The air grew colder, and she wrapped her coat tighter around herself, the fabric providing little comfort against the chill seeping into her bones.

Her phone buzzed in her pocket, a sudden intrusion into the quiet. She pulled it out, glancing at the screen. A message from her assistant, reminding her of a meeting later in the day. She typed a quick reply, assuring him she'd be back in time, and slipped the phone away. Her focus needed to be here, now.

The station's main hall loomed ahead, its grand arches still hinting at the elegance that once was. She walked slowly, her footsteps echoing through the vast space. Every corner seemed to whisper secrets, every shadow a reminder of the past. She stopped in the center, turning slowly, taking it all in.

A flicker of movement caught her eye. She turned sharply, heart pounding. Nothing. Just the trick of light playing on her nerves, she told herself. Yet, the sense of being watched persisted, gnawing at her composure.

She approached the ticket counter, its wooden surface scarred and worn. Her fingers brushed against it, and she imagined her grandfather standing there, his smile bright and welcoming. She closed her eyes, the memories flooding back. He had been her hero, a pillar of strength and kindness. His death had shattered her, and the unanswered questions had left a void she had never been able to fill.

Claire's eyes snapped open as a loud creak echoed through the hall. She spun around, her breath catching in her throat. The massive doors at the far end of the hall, long sealed shut, had moved. She stared, heart racing, as they creaked open just a sliver, revealing a glimpse of darkness beyond.

Summoning every ounce of courage, she walked towards the doors, each step measured and deliberate. Her hand reached out, pushing them open wider. The room beyond was shrouded in darkness, the faint light from the hall barely penetrating the gloom. She hesitated on the threshold, the sense of foreboding almost overwhelming.

Taking a deep breath, she stepped inside. The air was colder here, the smell of damp and decay stronger. Her eyes adjusted slowly to the dim light, and she could make out shapes—old furniture, covered in dust and cobwebs, remnants of a time long past.

Something glinted in the corner, catching her attention. She moved closer, her heart pounding louder with each step. It was a mirror, its surface cracked and tarnished, but reflecting just enough light to reveal the faint outline of something behind her.

Claire turned slowly, dread coiling in her stomach. The outline became clearer—a figure standing just outside the door she had entered. Her breath hitched, fear paralyzing her for a moment.

"Who's there?" she called out, her voice steady despite the terror gripping her.

No response. The figure didn't move, didn't react. She took a tentative step forward, straining to see through the darkness. Another step, and the figure dissolved into the shadows, leaving her alone once more.

Heart still racing, she backed away, her mind spinning with questions. What had she seen? Was her mind playing tricks on her, or was something more sinister at play?

Determined to find answers, Claire turned back to the mirror. In its cracked surface, she saw herself—worn, but resolute. This was her chance to uncover the truth, to finally put her grandfather's ghost to rest. She couldn't let fear stop her now.

With renewed determination, she left the dark room, the sense of foreboding still heavy but her resolve stronger. She had a station to revive, a mystery to solve, and a past to confront. The shadows of the past would not hold her back. Not anymore.

As she stepped back into the main hall, her phone buzzed again. This time, it was her business partner, David.

"Claire, are you there?" David's voice crackled through the speaker.

"Yes, I'm here," she replied, her voice echoing slightly in the vast space.

"How's it looking? Worth the investment?"

Claire glanced around, taking in the decaying grandeur. *"It's going to need a lot of work, David. But yes, I think it's worth it."*

David chuckled. *"I trust your instincts. You've always had an eye for potential. But are you sure this is a good idea? Given the... history?"*

Claire paused, the weight of her decision settling over her. *"I need to do this, David. For my grandfather. For my family. And for myself."*

There was a moment of silence on the other end. "Alright," David said finally. *"Just be careful, okay? That place gives me the creeps."*

Claire smiled despite herself. *"Thanks, David. I will."*

After ending the call, she wandered deeper into the station. The once bustling platforms were now silent, the tracks overgrown with weeds. She could almost hear the distant echoes of train whistles and bustling crowds, a stark contrast to the eerie silence now.

She made her way to her grandfather's old office, tucked away in a corner of the station. The door was slightly ajar, and she hesitated before pushing it open. The room was exactly as she remembered it from her childhood visits—a wooden desk, shelves lined with books and ledgers, a dusty old typewriter in the corner.

Claire stepped inside, running her fingers over the desk's worn surface. Her grandfather had been a meticulous man, and his office reflected that. Everything had its place, from the neatly stacked papers to the pens lined up in a row. She pulled open a drawer, revealing more papers, yellowed with age.

As she rifled through the documents, a folded piece of paper caught her eye. She unfolded it carefully, revealing a map of the station. Her grandfather's neat handwriting marked various points of interest, including a small, hidden room she had never noticed before.

Intrigued, she traced the route with her finger, committing it to memory. This hidden room could hold the answers she was seeking. She left the office, the map clutched tightly in her hand, and made her way towards the location indicated.

The path led her through narrow corridors and up a set of rickety stairs. The station's upper levels were even more decrepit, the air thick with dust and the scent of decay. Finally, she reached a small, nondescript door, almost hidden behind a stack of old crates.

Taking a deep breath, Claire pushed the door open. The room beyond was small and cramped, filled with old files and boxes. She began to sift through the contents, her heart pounding with anticipation.

Hours passed as she searched, the daylight fading into twilight. Just as she was about to give up, her fingers brushed against a small, leather-bound journal. She pulled it out, her breath catching as she recognized her grandfather's handwriting.

With trembling hands, she opened the journal, the pages filled with notes and observations. One entry in particular caught her eye, dated just a week before his death.

"Suspicions grow stronger. Something is not right. Must investigate further, but danger looms. Trust no one."

Claire's heart raced as she read the words. Her grandfather had known something, something that had ultimately led to his death. She needed to uncover the truth, to finish what he had started.

Just as she closed the journal, a sudden noise made her jump. Footsteps echoed in the corridor outside, growing louder with each passing second. She froze, the journal clutched to her chest, as the door slowly creaked open.

A man's silhouette filled the doorway, backlit by the dim light from the hall. Claire's heart pounded in her chest, the journal pressed against her. "*Who are you?*" she demanded, her voice trembling slightly.

The figure stepped forward, revealing a tall, older man with sharp features and piercing blue eyes. He wore a long coat, its dark fabric swirling around his legs as he moved. "*My name is Henry Fletcher,*" he said, his voice deep and calm. "*I used to work here.*"

Claire's mind raced. "*Henry Fletcher... the retired detective?*"

Henry nodded, a faint smile touching his lips. "*That's right. I've been keeping an eye on this place, and on you, Miss Kensington. I know why you're here.*"

Claire's grip on the journal tightened. "*Then you know about my grandfather.*"

Henry's expression softened. "*Yes. I knew him well. We were friends, and his death... it has haunted me for years.*"

Claire took a step forward, her curiosity piqued. "*You must know something, then. Something that can help me.*"

Henry glanced around the room before meeting her gaze. "*I do. But it's not safe to discuss it here. There are eyes everywhere.*"

A chill ran down Claire's spine. *"What do you mean? Who's watching?"*

Henry moved closer, his voice dropping to a whisper. *"There are people who don't want the truth to come out. People who will do anything to keep it buried. Meet me at the old café down the street in an hour. We'll talk there."*

Before she could respond, Henry turned and left, his footsteps echoing down the corridor. Claire stood frozen for a moment, the weight of his words sinking in. She had to know more, to uncover the secrets that had claimed her grandfather's life.

With the journal safely tucked into her bag, she made her way out of the station, her mind swirling with questions. The streets outside were bathed in the golden glow of the setting sun, the city's bustle a stark contrast to the eerie silence of the station.

The old café was a quaint, nostalgic place, its walls adorned with vintage photos and memorabilia. Claire found a quiet corner and ordered a cup of coffee, her thoughts racing as she waited for Henry.

He arrived precisely on time, his demeanor calm and composed. He slid into the seat across from her, his eyes scanning the room before settling on her. *"Thank you for meeting me,"* he said, his tone sincere.

Claire nodded, leaning forward. *"Tell me everything you know, Mr. Fletcher. I need to understand what happened to my grandfather."*

Henry took a deep breath, his eyes darkening with old memories. *"Your grandfather was a good man, Miss Kensington. He discovered something at that station, something dangerous. He confided in me, but before we could act, he was killed."*

Claire's heart ached at the thought. *"What did he find?"*

Henry hesitated, choosing his words carefully. *"There was a group—powerful, influential people—using the station for illegal activities. Smuggling, black market deals, even drug trafficking. Your grandfather stumbled upon their operation and tried to expose them."*

A wave of nausea washed over Claire. *"And they killed him to keep him quiet."*

Henry nodded grimly. *"Yes. And they've kept a close watch on the station ever since, to ensure no one else uncovers their secrets."*

Claire's resolve hardened. *"We have to expose them, Mr. Fletcher. For my grandfather, and for everyone else they've hurt."*

Henry's eyes held a mixture of respect and caution. *"It won't be easy. They're dangerous, and they won't hesitate to eliminate anyone who threatens them. But if you're willing to take the risk, I'll help you."*

Claire's gaze was steady. "*I am. Whatever it takes.*"

Henry nodded, a glint of determination in his eyes. "*Then we need to be careful, gather evidence, and build a case strong enough to bring them down. And we need to find allies—people who can help us.*"

Claire thought of the journal, the cryptic notes her grandfather had left behind. "*I found this,*" she said, pulling it from her bag. "*My grandfather's journal. There might be clues in here.*"

Henry took the journal, flipping through its pages. "*This is a good start. We'll go through it together, find out what he knew, and follow the leads. But remember, we're treading on dangerous ground. Trust no one outside our circle.*"

Claire nodded, the weight of their task settling over her. "*I understand.*"

As they left the café, the sun had set, casting long shadows over the streets. Claire felt a renewed sense of purpose, a determination to see this through, no matter the cost. The shadows of the past were dark and treacherous, but with Henry's help, she would uncover the truth and bring light to the darkness.

The journey had begun, and there was no turning back.

Chapter 2: Echoes in the Halls

Claire Kensington exited the café, the chill of the evening air wrapping around her like a shroud. The streets were less crowded now, the fading light casting long, eerie shadows that seemed to follow her every move. She clutched her grandfather's journal tightly, the weight of its secrets pressing down on her. Henry Fletcher's presence beside her was both comforting and unsettling; his knowledge of the station's dark past meant he was as much a part of the mystery as the station itself.

As they walked back to the station, the silence between them was thick with unspoken thoughts. Claire's mind raced, trying to piece together the fragments of her grandfather's life and untimely death. The station loomed ahead, its decaying structure a stark reminder of the journey she was about to undertake.

Henry broke the silence first. *"We need to be cautious, Claire. The people we're up against won't hesitate to silence anyone who gets too close."*

Claire nodded, her resolve unshaken. *"I understand. But I have to know the truth. My grandfather deserves justice."*

Henry's eyes softened with a mix of admiration and concern. *"Then we'll proceed carefully. We'll start by exploring the station, room by room. There might be more clues hidden in the places your grandfather frequented."*

They arrived at the station's entrance, the heavy gate still ajar from Claire's earlier visit. As they stepped inside, the oppressive silence greeted them once more. The main hall was bathed in the dim glow of the setting sun, casting long shadows that danced across the cracked tiles and broken benches.

Henry led the way, his flashlight cutting through the darkness. Claire followed closely, her eyes scanning every corner for signs of her grandfather's presence. They moved through the main hall, their footsteps echoing eerily in the vast space. Every sound seemed amplified, the creaks and groans of the old building unsettling Claire's nerves.

As they ventured deeper into the station, the flickering lights and distant echoes began to play tricks on her mind. She saw fleeting shadows at the edge of her vision and heard whispers that seemed to come from the walls themselves. Her heart pounded in her chest, but she pushed the fear aside, determined to stay focused.

Henry stopped in front of a door marked "Records Room." He turned to Claire, his expression serious, the lines on his face deepening with determination. *"This is where your grandfather spent a lot of his time. If there are any clues, we'll find them here."*

Claire nodded, her heart racing with a mix of anticipation and anxiety. She took a deep breath as Henry pushed the door open. The room beyond was shrouded in shadows, illuminated only by the beam of Henry's flashlight. Dust particles floated lazily in the light, creating an ethereal dance in the air. The shelves that lined the walls were stacked with old ledgers, faded documents, and rows of photographs in tarnished frames. The air carried the heavy scent of aged paper and a faint hint of mildew, adding to the atmosphere of mystery that enveloped them.

They moved cautiously into the room, each step echoing softly against the worn wooden floor. The dim light cast eerie shadows, adding to the tension in the air. Claire's fingers brushed over the spines of ancient books, her eyes scanning the faded labels in search of something that might leap out at her. Dust motes danced in the slivers of light filtering through the grime-covered windows, adding to the sense of abandonment.

She pulled out a few ledgers, their pages brittle and yellowed with age, flipping through them with a mixture of hope and apprehension. Each page turned crackled softly, the faint smell of old paper filling the air. Claire's heart raced as she scanned the names and numbers, searching for a clue that would tie everything together.

Meanwhile, Henry's attention was drawn to a sturdy filing cabinet nestled in the corner, half-hidden by shadows. With careful precision, he began to open drawer after drawer, the metal sliding noiselessly despite its age. Each folder he retrieved was handled with the utmost care, as though he feared disturbing the secrets they held.

"Your grandfather was meticulous in his record-keeping," he remarked softly, his voice barely above a whisper, betraying both reverence and a hint of concern. His eyes darted between the documents and Claire, the weight of their discovery pressing heavily on them.

Claire nodded, her fingers trembling slightly as she continued to sift through the ledgers. *"He knew this day might come,"* she murmured, almost to herself. The room seemed to close in on them, the silence amplifying the sound of their breathing and the rustle of paper.

Suddenly, Claire's hand froze on a page filled with familiar names and dates. *"Henry, look at this,"* she whispered urgently. Henry moved to her side, peering over her shoulder at the ledger. His eyes widened as he took in the information, a mixture of excitement and dread crossing his features.

"This... this could be it," he breathed, his voice tinged with awe.

But before they could delve deeper, a faint creak echoed from the hallway outside. Claire and Henry exchanged a quick, tense glance. The sound of approaching footsteps grew louder, more deliberate.

"Quick, put everything back," Henry hissed, his hands moving swiftly to replace the files and close the drawers. Claire shoved the ledgers back onto the shelf, her movements frantic yet careful not to leave any sign of their intrusion.

They backed away from the cabinet, their hearts pounding in unison. The footsteps stopped just outside the door, and a shadow loomed through the crack under the door.

Claire held her breath, her eyes locked on the doorknob as it began to turn slowly.

Claire glanced over at him, her curiosity piqued even further. *"What's in there?"* she asked, her voice barely audible in the stillness of the room.

Henry hesitated for a moment, then pulled out a folder labeled "Confidential." Its cover was worn and weathered, the contents within hinting at a history that was both intriguing and potentially perilous. With a steady hand, he opened it, revealing a collection of photographs and meticulously written notes. Claire leaned in closer, her eyes widening as she recognized familiar faces captured in moments that seemed innocuous yet held an undeniable weight of significance.

"It looks like surveillance photos," Henry murmured, his voice tinged with solemnity. *"These are dated just before your grandfather's death."*

Claire's breath caught in her throat as she studied the images, her mind racing with questions. Who had been watching her grandfather? And why? The room seemed to close in around them, the stillness broken only by the faint hum of distant traffic outside. Each photograph told a story, but whether it was one of danger or revelation, they were yet to uncover.

Claire moved closer, her eyes widening as she recognized some of the faces in the photographs. *"These people... they're all prominent figures in the community. Why would my grandfather have these?"*

Henry's brow furrowed as he examined the notes. *"He must have been onto something big. These notes suggest he was gathering evidence of illegal activities."*

A chill ran down Claire's spine. *"And he was killed to keep it all quiet."*

Henry nodded, *"It seems so. But these notes are incomplete. We need to find the rest of his research if we're going to expose the truth."*

Claire's determination hardened. *"Then we keep looking. There has to be more."*

They continued their search, the sense of unease growing with each passing minute. The station seemed to come alive around them, the flickering lights casting ominous shadows on the walls. Claire's mind raced with questions, each one leading to more uncertainty.

As they sifted through the records, Claire's thoughts drifted back to her childhood visits to the station. She remembered her grandfather's warm smile, the way he would lift her up to see the trains arriving and departing. Those memories felt like a lifetime ago, now overshadowed by the dark secrets they were uncovering.

A sudden noise made Claire jump, her heart pounding in her chest. She turned to see Henry standing still, his flashlight beam focused on a spot in the corner of the room. *"What is it?"* she whispered, moving closer.

Henry pointed to a loose floorboard, slightly raised from the others. "Look at this."

Claire knelt down, her fingers prying at the edge of the loose floorboard. It came up easily, revealing a small, dust-covered compartment underneath. Inside, she found a bundle of papers, tied together with a piece of fraying twine.

She pulled them out, her hands trembling with a mix of anticipation and fear. *"These must be his notes. The missing pieces."*

Henry leaned over her shoulder, his breath warm against her ear as his eyes scanned the documents. *"This is it, Claire. This is what we need to bring them down."*

Claire's heart raced as she flipped through the pages, each one filled with her grandfather's meticulous handwriting. He had documented everything—names, dates, transactions. It was all here, the evidence they needed to expose the criminals who had taken his life.

A chill ran down her spine as she absorbed the magnitude of what they had discovered. But just as they were beginning to comprehend the full extent of the information, the sound of footsteps echoed through the hallway outside.

Claire and Henry exchanged a tense glance, their senses on high alert. The footsteps grew louder, more deliberate. Someone was coming.

Henry quickly gathered the papers, tucking them into his coat. *"We need to leave. Now."*

Claire's mind raced, searching for a way out. The only exit was the door they had entered through, but the footsteps were drawing closer, accompanied by muffled voices.

"Wait," she whispered, her voice barely audible. She scanned the room, her eyes falling on a small window high on the wall. *"There, the window."*

Henry nodded, his face set in determination. He gave her a boost, and she scrambled through, her heart pounding in her chest. Henry followed, just as the door to the room creaked open.

They landed in a narrow alleyway, the cool night air hitting their faces. Without a word, they ran, the weight of the evidence heavy in Henry's coat, and the specter of their pursuers never far behind.

Claire nodded, her pulse quickening. They moved swiftly, exiting the records room and making their way back through the labyrinthine corridors. The footsteps grew louder, and closer, as if someone was following them.

They reached the main hall, the oppressive silence broken only by their hurried breaths. Just as they neared the exit, a figure emerged from the shadows, blocking their path.

"Going somewhere?" a voice sneered, cold and menacing.

Claire's heart sank as she recognized the man—a local politician with a reputation for corruption. He stepped forward, flanked by two burly men who looked ready for a fight.

Henry stepped protectively in front of Claire, his expression hard. *"We're leaving. Step aside."*

The politician laughed, a cruel sound that echoed through the hall. *"I don't think so. You've been poking around where you don't belong. It's time you learned a lesson."*

Claire's mind raced, searching for a way out. They were trapped, outnumbered, and unarmed. But she refused to let fear paralyze her. Her grandfather's legacy depended on their survival.

Henry's voice was steady, unwavering. *"You don't want to do this. We have evidence. If anything happens to us, it will come to light."*

The politician's smile faltered, uncertainty flickering in his eyes. But he quickly recovered, his expression hardening. *"Hand over the documents, and we might let you walk out of here."*

Claire's grip on Henry's arm tightened, her resolve strengthening. *"We're not giving you anything."*

Henry's grip on Claire's hand tightened. She could feel his resolve, his silent determination not to give in. They exchanged a quick glance, a mutual understanding passing between them.

"You'll have to take them from us," Henry said, his voice low and defiant.

The politician's eyes narrowed. *"Very well,"* he hissed, signaling his men.

As the burly men advanced, Claire's mind raced. There had to be a way out. She scanned the room, her eyes landing on a heavy iron candlestick on a nearby table. She subtly gestured to it, and Henry gave a slight nod.

Just as the first thug reached them, Henry lunged for the candlestick, swinging it with all his might. The thug staggered back, clutching his head. Claire seized the moment, kicking the other man in the knee, causing him to crumple to the ground.

The tension in the air was palpable, the standoff teetering on the edge of violence. Just as the situation seemed about to explode, a sudden noise echoed through the hall—the distant wail of sirens, growing louder with each passing second.

"Run!" Henry shouted, grabbing her hand.

They dashed towards the exit, hearts pounding, the politician's angry shouts echoing behind them. They burst through the door and into the night, adrenaline propelling them forward. The evidence was still safe, and so were they—for now. But Claire knew this was just the beginning. The truth about her grandfather's death was within reach, and she would stop at nothing to uncover it.

The politician's eyes widened in panic. *"Cops! We need to go."*

He and his men fled, disappearing into the shadows. Claire and Henry stood frozen for a moment, the adrenaline still coursing through their veins.

Henry's voice broke the silence. *"We need to get out of here before they come back."*

Claire nodded, her heart still racing. They hurried out of the station, the cold night air a welcome relief from the oppressive atmosphere inside.

As they walked away, Claire couldn't help but feel a mix of triumph and fear. They had found the evidence, but the danger was far from over. The shadows of the past still loomed large, and their enemies would stop at nothing to keep their secrets hidden.

But Claire was determined. With Henry by her side, she would uncover the truth and bring justice to her grandfather's memory. The echoes in the halls of the old station had revealed their first clues, but the journey was only beginning.

Chapter 3: The First Revelation

Claire couldn't sleep that night. Even after getting home and checking her locks several times to ensure no one could get inside, she couldn't help but feel paranoid. She could still remember the sneer on the guy's face as he threatened them. The adrenaline in her body had spiked in that moment, pushing her into a fight or flight mode.

The truth is that Claire thought that she was prepared for what came with the risk of uncovering the truth, but it wasn't until she was in that situation with people charging at her did it hit her just how dangerous this could be. But that didn't mean that she was going to back out. Rather, this gave her an idea of what she had gotten herself into.

Her grandfather meant a lot to her, and even though she was terrified like anyone would be after the encounter she just had, she was still determined to find the truth and bring justice to her grandfather. If there was one thing she had learned from him, it was to always fight for what was right. But she still couldn't help but feel grateful for the fact that Henry was with her.

If she was alone, they could have overpowered her and taken the evidence from her. Just the thought of that concerned Claire. She stared up at the ceiling, her mind crowded with too many thoughts for her to be able to sleep. All she could think about was the documents they had discovered and the events that had taken place that day.

The first thing Claire had done when she got home was hide those documents. Her paranoia did not let her rest until she was sure that the documents were hidden and out of anyone's reach. Who knew what could happen? If anyone found a way to infiltrate her house, she needed to make sure they didn't get their hands on those documents. If those documents were gone, she would be left with nothing, steering her back to the first stage.

But now, after all these hours, Claire was starting to accept that the troubles for the night were over. Slowly, she got up accepting defeat. It was going to be a sleepless night, followed by god knows how many more with the ways things were now. Claire wasn't sure if she would ever feel safe again, but she hoped that once she found out the truth and exposed it she could put this behind her and move on.

She walked over to the corner of her room. Sweeping an eye around the room once more, suspiciously, she ensured that all curtains were done and there was no way for anyone to see inside her room. Slowly, she sunk down on her knees, grabbing onto the loose floorboard under the fluffy carpet that she had used to hide the documents.

The feeling of déjà vu hit her suddenly as she remembered her childhood. It was his grandfather who had found her in this hiding spot. All through her childhood, Claire would hide candies and video games that she didn't want her mom to take away from her. She couldn't believe that it had come to the point when she was hiding truly confidential documents, that could mean everything in there.

She pulled the stack of documents out, taking them back to her bed as she looked over them. When they found those documents first, they only had enough time to skim through them. But now, Claire could finally properly go through these documents and uncover all the secrets and information hidden within. The weight of the pages felt heavier than it should, pressing down on her.

Claire carefully untied the fraying twine once more. She watched as her fingers trembled, unable to control her reaction. She still hadn't fully recovered from the adrenaline rush and having something so important in her hand made her even more nervous. This document right here could change everything. She handled the fragile pages carefully, not wanting to accidentally tear them. She shifted in her place, spreading the pages open on the bed as the story that they held slowly began to unfold.

When Henry and her had skimmed through it they didn't get a lot of time to truly read all the contents, so as Claire looked down upon one of the handwritten letters in the papers she picked it up. Her eyes skimmed through the contents as she read the letter addressed to a well-known local politician that Claire remembered hearing from.

Claire could practically hear her grandfather's tone as she read his words. The letter was filled with the details of all the allegations and information that he had found about the corruption and illegal activities taking place in the railway station. Just reading about what was going on, she could get an idea of just how mad her grandfather would have been. If there was anything he hated it was corruption.

She put the letter away, continuing to look through the other things. Ignoring the pictures for a moment, she reached for something she hadn't seen before. Moving the pictures away, she found a detailed map of the town. Confused, for a moment as to why her grandfather would have a map of the whole town, Claire took a closer look at the map and saw several places on the map being circled and written over.

Claire squinted her eyes, trying to read the small handwriting on the map near all the circled places. It took her a moment to realize that the places that had been highlighted were the places where her grandfather had encountered criminal activities. She felt a wave of pride wash over her. Not only had her grandfather been able to uncover the truth but he had also managed to do thorough research, putting his life in jeopardy in the process.

It killed her to know that even after everything, he still hadn't been able to finish what he started. The fact that his enemies got to him before he could expose them made Claire feel angry. But that didn't matter any longer because she was going to end this for her. Her grandfather's death wouldn't be in vain.

She couldn't wait to discuss everything with Henry. After escaping, Henry dropped her off at home and promised to come over tomorrow. They had agreed to keep their head down and stay inside until they felt safe enough to go out. She just hoped that he had gotten home safe and no more trouble had come his way. She was grateful for his support and help, without him Claire would be lost.

Claire continued to study the map, trying to see the places and see if she could find anything that she could recognize. She didn't even realize when her eyes got heavy and drifted close as she fell asleep. Overcome with exhaustion and the aftermath of all that adrenaline, Claire fell asleep right there with all the documents scattered around it.

The next morning, Claire woke up to the incessant ringing of her doorbell. She jerked away, her heart instantly pounding as she jumped out of bed in panic. Her eyes strayed toward all the scattered documents and she cursed internally. What if someone had found her and was trying to get in and steal these documents?

Her mind raced as she thought of what to do. She wasn't sure if she had enough time to hide the documents again, so instead she gathered them and hid them under her mattress before rushing toward the door. She paused to grab a knife and her pepper spray just in case something went wrong. She could feel her heartbeat, the thunderous beat of it was the only thing she could hear in the silence as she approached the door.

She stayed silent as she peeked into the eyehole, trying to see how many people were outside. But when she peered out, she found Henry standing there looking around nervously. With a sigh of relief, Claire swung the door open.

"Henry, thank god it's you." She said as she beckoned him inside and instantly locked the door.

"I am sorry if I alerted you. I was trying not to linger outside for too long." He said apologetically.

"It's fine, I just wanted to be safe." She said as she led him to her room.

"Did you run into any trouble after last night?" Henry asked her, his voice tinged with concern.

"No, thankfully nobody followed me home. I was so paranoid I couldn't sleep though so I decided to take a deeper look into the documents that we found." She said as she shook her head.

"And did you find anything new?" Henry asked, his eyebrow raised to which Claire instantly nodded as she moved to grab the documents from under the mattress.

"That's a very original place to hide papers," Henry quipped, amusement evident in his voice and Claire couldn't help but roll her eyes light-heartedly.

"I didn't have much time to hide since someone was ringing the bell quite incessantly." She retorted making him chuckle.

"You are truly his granddaughter," Henry said softly and Claire's expression softened too. She gave him a sad smile at that.

They stayed silent for a few minutes as Claire found the papers and spread them out once more for Henry to see.

"Grandpa not only knew about whatever illegal activities that were going on but he also made it his mission to uncover every detail regarding that. He even wrote a letter, telling a politician everything that he had discovered." She told him as she showed him the letter.

Henry read it quickly, his expression turning serious as he read the contents of the letter. Once done, he looked up at Claire with a grim expression on his face.

"He sacrificed his life trying to expose them." He said sorrowfully and Claire's heart clenched as she nodded.

"These are some very serious accusations, if he had gone public with these he would have caused a huge scandal. All these corrupt people would have panicked and tried everything to shut him up." She said, wishing that her grandfather hadn't met such a fate.

"You are right," Henry said quietly.

"That's not all. I found a few more images and the people's faces are clearer in these ones. It seems like Grandpa took these pictures himself. He must have snuck into these secret meetings. There are pictures of so many things, even money being exchanged." Claire shared with Henry as she showed him the pictures and he looked at them carefully.

"The fact that he chose to put his own life in danger and take these pictures himself means that he couldn't have trusted anyone else, not even the authorities," Henry said after a moment and Claire realized he was right.

"What if the authorities were *involved too?"* Claire voiced out and Henry's lips thinned.

"It's possible." He admitted. *"Your grandfather was clearly collecting evidence on his own, it must have taken him years to compile all this."* He said.

"I also found a map in which he circled several places. From what I can understand those are all places where illegal activity was taking place. I want you to take a look and see if you can recognize any of those places." She mentioned as she pulled the map out and showed it to him.

Claire watched as he carefully looked at the map and all its markings before he finally spoke.

"I can recognize a few places. There is the station," he told her as he pointed at it on the map before continuing. *"That's the*

warehouse near the docks, one of the nearby warehouses, and..." he paused suddenly making Claire tense.

"*What?*" she asked, concerned.

"*Isn't this your family house?*" Henry asked hesitantly, pointing at one of the circled places on the map.

Claire's eyes widened as she realized he was right. "*Why would he mark our house?*" she asked, her eyes wide and Henry shook his head, unsure.

"*He must have found something there.*" He murmured as he continued looking at the map.

Claire sat there silently, digesting the fact that this whole mess had been extended to her house. Once Henry was done, he looked up at her.

"*We need to talk to someone who knew your* Grandfather *most, and was with him the most in his final days.*" He said.

"*But who?*" Claire questioned.

"*One of his colleagues. Give me a few days, I will get in contact with him and let you know. Till then stay safe okay?*" he said and she had barely nodded before he was gone, leaving her alone to deal with all the bombs that had been dropped today.

Chapter 4: Whispers of Betrayal

The next few days passed torturously slow. Claire felt caged, almost as if she had been caught by someone and had no escape. Her house had never felt more suffocating before. But the outside seemed just as scary. It was like being stuck in a maze with no escape and the haunting thud of someone's feet as they followed her.

Over the past few days, Claire had become more paranoid than ever. It was as if the quiet, haunting aura of the railway had followed her home. Once a comfortable place, her house was nothing more than a place filled with shadows and the lurking presence of something she couldn't see. She wasn't sure if it was just her and her fears taking over or if there was something strange that was happening.

Claire was quite used to living alone, having moved out of her family house at a young age. And never had she ever found herself being this scared of being alone. But somehow, she couldn't shake the feeling that somebody or something was constantly watching her as if keeping an eye on her.

Even now, as she lay on her bed, she felt the heavy feeling of somebody peeking down at her. She tossed and turned, getting up several times to ensure she had locked all gates and windows and made sure the curtains were all drawn. She had done everything in the past few days to ensure that nobody could come in or even see inside her house.

Ever since Henry's last visit and cryptic parting words, she hadn't heard from him. At first, she assumed that he was taking his time tracking down; however, he thought he would be able to help them out, but now she couldn't help but feel concerned. Was he even okay? What if somebody got to him and hurt him in any way? And most importantly, how would she know?

It was only after Henry had left that Claire realized she had no way of contacting Henry. Both their meetings had been so urgent and concerning that they didn't even remember to exchange numbers, and with each passing day that Henry didn't stop by, she got more and more worried.

She had been locked inside her house for too long and knew that she would eventually have to leave the house. But the thought of walking out of her house, unprotected and unaware of what happened made chills go down Claire's body. Even now, as she lay on her bed, in the safety of the house, she couldn't help but feel tense and edgy, as if there was something threatening her.

Not only did the house feel creepy, but the weight of the documents still sat heavy in her mind, making it impossible for her to stop thinking and obsessing over what she had learned. She spent days reading and going over the documents again and again to see if she missed something. As she lay in bed, trying desperately to fall asleep, she thought of everything she had found until finally, sleep overtook her, but it was anything but restful.

The sound of the trains passing was deafening. In the quiet, dark night the sound of the trains passing through the railway was loud enough to fill the air. Claire stood there, in the heart of the station and when she turned around to face the track and see the trains that were making all the noise, she found nothing there.

Suddenly, the night became eerily still and silent, filled with an unnatural chill that made chills run down her body. The silence was creepy, Claire thought. She could only hear the faint whisper of the wind occasionally, which made her pause every time. But there was something that beckoned her deeper into the station.

She didn't know what, but the urge to walk inside, to find something that called out to her, was too hard to resist as Claire started to take tentative steps leading her deeper into the station. A part of Claire's brain was yelling at her to stop, to turn around and walk away from the scene, choosing self-preservation, but the curious part of her that wanted to find what was inside and what called to her won as she kept walking.

As she kept moving, she felt the shadows move around her from the corner of her vision, making her breath hitch. She tried to tell herself it was just her paranoia making her feel like that and convinced herself to keep going until she felt a looming presence behind her, making her pause, rooted to the floor as she felt herself getting paralyzed from fear.

“Claire…” *a soft voice whispered directly into her ear, making her heart pound. Her fight and flight instinct was activated, but the soft voice in her ear made her pause. The sound was so foreign and yet unmistakable.*

“Grandpa…” *she murmured as she turned around as fast as she could, but the looming presence disappeared as she turned around. She looked around, trying desperately to find the source of the voice, but there was nothing there but empty air. She suddenly felt hyperaware.*

That voice, so soft and familiar, was her Grandfather’s, and she knew it. It felt comforting even in these unsettling surroundings; something about it felt soothing, almost as if he was here to reassure her. But no matter how much she tried to find him, she couldn’t see anything.

Determined to find him, Claire started walking again. She was convinced that her Grandfather was there and wanted her to find him. But as she crossed the distance and walked in deeper, the darkness grew, engulfing her in it. Suddenly, Claire could feel several presences near her, but none of them felt safe and comfortable like before.

Her eyes roamed, trying to find any light, when she saw a small dim light at the end of the hallway she was on. She rushed toward it just as she saw a shadowy form slip between the door at the end of the hallway.

"Grandpa!" *she shouted as she ran toward the door, but the minute she reached the end of the hallway, the door disappeared, and she felt the ghostly figures begin to materialize all around her. She could feel herself panic as she watched the figures lurking all around her. They moved in and out of shadows as she caught a glimpse of their faces, contorted with pain and sorrow that looked ghastly.*

Claire could feel her heart pounding in her chest as she looked at the ghostly creatures in front. She wanted to look away and run far far away from all of this but something anchored her there, making her unable to look away from what she saw. Out of nowhere, the ghosts started to yowl, their voices filled with agony as if someone was burning them alive. They screeched loud enough to make Claire cover her face.

She ducked as all the ghosts turned at once and floated toward a door that had just appeared. There was an urgency on their hollow faces as they swarmed toward the door, and even Claire wanted to run away from all of this; one of the ghosts grabbed her wrist, making her mouth fly open in a scream.

But no voice escaped her as she panicked. But the constant tug on her wrist made her give in as she was dragged along with the rest of the creatures. She felt like she was in a daze, everything seemed hazy and when she blinked her eyes open all the creatures she could see before had vanished, and now she stood in an empty chamber that echoed the sound of her breathing.

She looked around, unable to comprehend what was going on. She turned around, about to call out for help when suddenly she saw somebody standing a few feet away from her. The man had his back to her, but she didn't need him to turn to recognize him.

"Claire, I knew you would make it." *Her grandfather's voice was the same, yet somehow different, as if he was speaking from across some wind barrier.*

"Grandpa, what is going on? Where have you gone?" *Claire asked, her emotions crowding her as she finally spoke to him.*

"I am so proud of you, Claire. I wish I could have been there, but I can't." *Claire's heart ached at the familiarity in his voice, the pride as he told her how he felt. He had often told her how proud he was of her, and it felt like an eternity had passed since she heard those words from him.*

"Where have you gone, Grandpa? What happened to you?" *Claire asked as she tried to take a step forward but found herself unable to move.*

"*I* am sorry I have left such a big task for you. I am sorry that I am not there for you. But I have faith in you, my Claire. You can do what I can't." *Claire could feel tears of frustration and angst build in her eyes as she kept trying to go to him, but no* matter *how much she tried, she just couldn't.*

"Grandpa, why won't you turn around? Please, I need you. I know you think I can do this, and I am trying, but I don't know what to do. I don't know what to look for." *Claire said, desperation bleeding into her voice. She wanted to see him and hug him once more.*

"You already have all you need, my dear. You just need to look deeper. Look for my words, Claire. My words will guide you." *As her Grandfather spoke, he started to walk away from her, and Claire couldn't help but jump.*

"Grandpa! No, wait! Please don't go! Please come back, please!" *Claire pleaded, her shouts getting louder as he kept walking away, and her desperation to run after him grew.*

She tried, pushing herself as much as she could to be able to move, and the more effort she put in, the more pain she felt until she let out a scream filled with pain.

"GRANDPA!" Claire woke up screaming, yelling for her Grandfather. She was covered in sweat, and her sheets were completely rumpled from her thrashing. She was breathing heavily as she came back to reality, blinking several times to fight off her disorientation.

As she tried to calm her breathing, she thought of what she saw. The dream felt too real, too vivid. There was something about the dream that made her feel like she needed to do something. Her Grandfather's words swarmed in her head as she repeated them.

"You already have all you need, my dear. You just need to look deeper. Look for my words, Claire. My words will guide you." She murmured the words again as if they had been seared into her head.

Her mind raced as she tried to make sense of the cryptic words. What was she missing? She had gone through all the documents, but there weren't many words from her Grandfather. She racked her brain until suddenly it hit her.

Without wasting a moment, Claire jumped out of bed and ran toward the floorboard, where she hid everything she had found at the station. She had been so focused on all the documents and evidence that they had found that she completely forgot about the journal she had found of her Grandfather.

She pulled the journal out with an urgency that she had never felt before. Opening it, she felt the texture of the yellow pages as she turned them. At first, she could see empty pages, making her urgency deflate and disappointment take over. But once she had reached the middle of the journal, she came across the familiar scrawl of her Grandfather's writing, making her eyes widen as she read the words.

July 1986

I am starting to think I am going crazy. Is this all in my head, or have I ventured too deep to turn back now? There is so much to uncover, and this odious business is too big. The more I find out, the worse it gets.

August 1986

I have started to feel like I am being followed. Either I have been discovered, or I am truly going crazy and seeing things that aren't there. I don't feel safe anywhere anymore. At the station, I feel like the shadows are moving.

August 1986

I have started leaving clues. I fear for my life now that I think I have been discovered. I know too much, and they know it. I have hidden clues in places only someone close to me would know to look in case I don't do the right thing; I hope someone else will do it for me.

December 1986

I finally have everything I need. I have all the evidence of this vile business; I am just waiting for the right time to come.

February 1987

Nowhere is safe.

May 1987

Trust no one. Friends turned into foes, danger all around.

June 1987

There is a mole. Somebody sold me out, feeding all the information to the wrong people. I don't know who it is yet, but I have my suspicions. I need to find the truth and the evidence. I pray that I am wrong, but I can't deny that someone close to me has betrayed me.

August 1987

I was right.

Claire couldn't help but gasp as she read the last entry. Her Grandfather had died in August 1987, which means that whoever had betrayed him was also responsible for his death.

Unable to come to terms with what she found out, Claire sat there, staring at the entries in the journal with disbelief.

Chapter 5: The Conspiracy Deepens

Claire had no idea how much time had passed as she sat there, shocked and confused at the same time. Everything she read and discovered from her grandfather's journal had sent her reeling. She knew that her grandfather had gotten involved in something dangerous; she also knew that something terrible had happened that caused his sudden death. But she had no idea that he had been betrayed by someone.

Just knowing that somebody close, somebody that her grandfather had trusted dearly, had betrayed him gnawed at her, twisting her thoughts into a dark spiral of suspicion and fear. She couldn't help but think of how he must have felt when he realized the truth. Her grandfather had been a smart but emotional man. His ability to sympathize and empathize with people was something Claire had always looked up to him for. But she realized now that maybe that quality had led him to his death.

She had no idea how to react to everything that she had just read. It was the middle of the night, and she was sitting on the floor with the journal on her lap. If the quietness in the house had bothered her before, it now felt downright oppressive. Not long ago, this house had been her only refuge, the only place she could always feel safe. But now, she felt as if the walls themselves were closing in with secrets she was only beginning to unearth.

She needed to discuss this with Henry and tell him about it. There were very few people that her grandfather trusted with everything, and it was clear that the person who had betrayed him was somebody close to him. So close that her grandfather had shared something so important and dangerous with them. Claire's heart ached at the thought. She couldn't help but think of how betrayed her grandfather would have felt when he found out that somebody he trusted so much had not only betrayed him but also become the cause of his death.

Anger ignited in Claire as she thought of the person who had betrayed her grandfather. If anything, this revelation further deepened her resolve to find the person who had caused this entire thing and was responsible for her grandfather's death. She was also determined to finish what her grandfather had started. If he planned to expose these corrupt public figures and put an end to this sick business, then that's what she would do.

The trouble was that she had no idea when Henry would return. It had already been days, and he had left with such a cryptic comment she was unsure if he would come back anytime soon. From what she could guess was that he was out searching for somebody. But who knew how long that would take, and Claire could no longer stay inside. She needed to get out, needed to do *something*.

She internally cursed as she remembered that she still hadn't gotten his contact information. She should have remembered to ask him, but they were so immersed in what they had found that it completely slipped her mind. And now she was once again stuck. The only thing she knew was that he worked somewhere near the café they had met up at.

She knew that the smart decision was to stay back home and wait for him. It was the smarter and safer option, but Claire could no longer stay inside. The house was becoming oppressive, and she knew that if she stayed inside any longer, she would drive herself crazy. But even as she made plans to leave, a feeling of dread settled in her stomach. The words from her grandfather's journal echoed in her mind: *Trust no one. Friends turned into foes, danger all around.*

It was scary leaving the house, but it was even more difficult to think of sitting back at home for a few more days. It had been a few days since Henry and she had been ambushed and threatened. It was obvious that there were people after both of them, but Claire would just have to be careful. She decided that tomorrow she would set out early when it was broad daylight and she was less likely to get attacked.

She planned to find Henry and go to the station. According to the journal, her grandfather had hidden important clues in that place, and she needed to find them if she planned to expose the people who were responsible for such horrible crimes. She felt like even though her grandfather hadn't said it, he had always expected me to be the one to finish this job for him.

We were always close, and he would always tell me how he trusted me to be able to do anything when I set my mind to it. And for so long, I doubted that, doubted if I could do anything meaningful. But he had been there every step of the way, motivating me, believing in me as he rooted for me. I am an agent today, a great one at that, because of him. It was his unrelenting support that made her come all this way, and now it was time for her to do something for him.

Claire checked the time and realized it was almost four a.m. If she planned to go out tomorrow, she needed to be alert and in the right state of mind. Even though she felt more awake than ever, she knew that she needed to sleep in order to be able to go out and look for answers tomorrow. With that thought in mind, she quickly hid everything again and went to bed, her grandfather's words the last thing on her mind as she drifted asleep.

The next morning, Claire wakes up to the sun shining down on her, filling her room with its bright rays. The dark and frightening aura of the room from last night had vanished. Getting out of bed, she checked the time to see if it was almost afternoon. Rushing to get ready, she jumped straight into the shower, all while her thoughts ran wild. She couldn't help but feel a little paranoid. She hadn't left the house in a few days, scared that somebody might hurt her.

As soon as she got out of the shower, she got dressed and instantly walked over to her nightstand, where she kept all her stuff. She pulled out a pocket knife, Taser, and pepper spray. She wished that she could have a proper weapon, but she didn't have many options right now. But she would rather have some semblance of safety than none at all.

With everything set, she took one last deep breath and left the safety of her house. As she ventured out, Claire tried to keep an eye on her surroundings, trying to be as careful as possible. She walked toward the cafe even as her nerves were on edge with every step she took. She tried to use streets that were crowded, avoiding any places that were quiet or isolated. But even then, she couldn't shake the feeling that she was being watched. She tried to brush off the paranoia, convincing herself it was just the lingering fear from her recent experiences. But as she walked, she caught glimpses of a shadowy figure trailing her at a distance, always staying just out of sight.

Claire's blood ran cold at sight, and without wasting a second, she started racing, being able to see the café she was trying to find. Soon, she was inside and surrounded by several people. She hadn't even noticed how breathless she was until she started to calm down. A few people gave her weird looks, and she ignored them as she took a seat at a nearby table.

She couldn't help but feel scared. She might be safe now, but how would she get home? What if they got to her and managed to get secrets out of me? She knew better than to underestimate the people that were after her. She held some very crucial evidence that could ruin several important figures, and she was sure they knew that.

Claire was so lost in her thoughts, trying to come up with a plan that would get her back home safely, that she didn't even notice when a man, almost the same age as her grandfather, took a seat at her table. As she noticed him, she flinched, a gasp escaping her as she tried to recover from the shock.

So much for being aware of your surroundings. A voice inside Claire's head taunted, and she grimaced. Pushing her unconscious self away, she took in the man in front of her.

The man looked suspicious, with eyes that seemed to hold many secrets and countless stories. There was something about him that made Claire's skin prickle, but it wasn't mainly negative. She couldn't help but feel like this man held the answers that she had been trying to seek. But she didn't give him the benefit of the doubt.

"Who are you?" Claire demanded.

"Are you sure that this is the right question? The more important question?" The man's voice was deep and gravelly as he dodged her question.

"What do you want?" Claire repeated, not putting her guard down.

"I have been looking for you," The man answered cryptically, raising her concerns even more.

"Why?" She asked. *"Who even are you, and how do you know me?"*

"That's not important," he said, leaning back as he looked me straight in the eye. *"What matters is that you're in grave danger. There are people who want to bury the secrets your grandfather uncovered, and they won't stop until they've silenced everyone who knows the truth."*

My eyes widened upon hearing his words; it was clear that this man knew something, but how? I look at him suspiciously. Somehow, this whole thing becomes more and more messy with every passing minute.

Chapter 6: Race Against Time

Claire stared at the man in front of her, feeling suspicious and curious at the same time. She had no idea who he was, where he had come from, and most importantly, if she could trust him. It was obvious that there were many people who would want to lure her into a trap. Threatening her hadn't worked, so maybe they were trying to trick her into handing over the evidence.

It was a dangerous game she was playing, one surrounding her with challenges and traps. She wondered if she truly could evade these and win in the end. But she would try, if not for her own sake then for her Grandfather's sake. And the man in front of her played some role in this twisted game that she didn't want to play but had to.

"And why should I trust you? You could be the one trying to harm me for all that I know." Claire remained confident, raising her eyebrow at him.

Her Grandfather had taught her to never let the other person see something they can use against her. It was true that she was confused and paranoid, but she wasn't about to let him take advantage of that.

"If you are smart, you won't make the mistake of trusting anyone. The mission that you have decided to take on is a

treacherous one, where you will find more enemies than friends. People die because they trust too much, too easily, and for your sake, I hope you are not stupid enough to do that." He answered in a dark tone, looking at her challengingly.

His words seemed too raw, too honest for her to doubt them. She had no idea who this man was, but he seemed to carry an air of confidence and a mask of mysteriousness that attracted attention. Whoever he was, he was involved in this messy situation, but the question was what side he was on.

"You keep talking in riddles, and I don't have time for that. If you don't have anything meaningful to say, I would rather be left alone." She told him crisply, and something gleamed in his eyes in response. It was not sinister but almost as if she had just drawn his interest.

"You have your grandfather's temperament, too, I can see." He muttered, and something about his words made her stomach flip.

"How did you know my grandfather?" Claire asked him, straightening. Could he be the one who betrayed him? The thought itself makes her get more alert. It was clear that whoever betrayed him was someone who knew him well, and with the ease and knowing glint in his eyes that he said that made it sound like he knew her Grandfather well.

"Of course I knew him. We were both part of something much larger than you can imagine, something that goes back decades,

maybe even centuries. If you think you know everything enough to be able to expose the truth, trust me, you don't. Your Grandfather stumbled upon a truth that powerful people have tried to keep hidden, and now they're after you because they think you might know what he did. And that should scare you." He said, his eyes darkening a little as his voice lowered.

"I don't care about the danger, but if there is anything that you can do to help me, let me know. You seem like you knew my Grandfather, which means you might know something else." Claire asked, leaning in. Maybe he could help her by telling her who her Grandfather was surrounded by.

"Your Grandfather was a man with many connections. Have you noticed how he was one of the most social people ever, having people around him whenever he was at the station? Don't you find it odd that somehow, the day he died, he was suddenly alone?" The man hints at something.

He is right, Claire thought. The station was always full, and she knew that someone was always keeping her grandfather company. Her heart raced as she understood what he was getting to.

"Do you know who was by his side the most?" Claire asked him, her heart beating loudly.

"I do," he says and my eyes start to widen when he continues, *"but I am afraid I can't tell you."* He finishes and all hope that she had felt growing, simmers down.

Claire couldn't bring herself to speak, to say anything for a moment. It is as if life has been playing with her, bringing her close to finding the truth and then pulling back immediately after.

"But," he speaks up again before she can respond and she looks up expectantly. *"what I can tell you is that there is somebody who was very close to your Grandfather, somebody you know very well. He is the one your Grandfather trusted the most."* He continued and Claire instantly perked up at the new information.

"I know him?" Claire asked again, confirming his words, but he silently nodded.

"Why should I trust you?" she demanded, even though she couldn't help but feel like this man was telling the truth. It made sense, but she prayed that her instinct wasn't leading her astray. Her Grandfather had always told her to trust her instinct, so that's what she was doing.

The man leaned back, a shadow crossing his face. *"You shouldn't. But if you want to survive long enough to find out what really happened to your Grandfather, you don't have much of a choice. From the way I see it, you have quite a lot of enemies and barely any allies. You would be stupid if you declined my help."*

Normally, such words would come with a considerable amount of smugness and arrogance. But as Claire searched the man's face she found nothing of that sort there. He looked serious, concerned even, if you had to assume. But not an ounce of smugness was visible on his face that showed that he had won some game he was playing and tricked her.

Her mind spun from everything that was happening. Every day she would come across a new detail that would alter the course of everything they had managed to figure out. She had no idea if she could trust this man in front of her, but she also knew that he was right. in the midst of juggling several enemies he and Henry had been the only two people who had come of use to her.

Before Claire could respond, the man slid a small, folded piece of paper across the table. *"This is all I can give you for now. If you want to know more, you'll have to look at the place where it all began. Places that you are most comfortable in and that you know well hold the biggest clues. But be careful—there are eyes everywhere."*

With that, the man stood up and walked away as if he had no idea who I was. The man disappeared the same way as he appeared, and Claire sat there for a few minutes trying to understand what had just happened. She looked down at the note in her hand, and with trembling fingers, she opened the small paper.

24.8615° N, 67.0099° E

Claire stared at the coordinates on the paper, trying to make sense of what it meant. Did these coordinates lead to something? Some proof? She knew that blindly trusting this man was dangerous; this could easily be a trap, and if she went along with it, she could risk not only her life but also all the evidence that her Grandfather had gathered. But something told her that this was her only lead, and if she wanted to find out the truth about her Grandfather's death, she had to follow it.

She sat there for a few minutes, trying to get her head together before she grabbed the paper and decided to leave. Leaving the cafe, she tried to become more aware of her surroundings. Her heart was still racing from the encounter with the strange man, and her thoughts were also jumbled. The weight of his cryptic warnings hung over her like a dark cloud, and every shadow seemed to hide another threat.

She crossed the street, lost in her mind as she tried to pull herself together when she bumped into someone. A scream builds in her throat, scared of getting ambushed. For a moment, she feared it might be another stranger sent to threaten her, but then she recognized Henry's familiar, worried eyes.

"Oh my god! Henry, thank god you are here!" Claire exclaimed, relieved to finally see him again.

"Is everything okay? I was so worried, Claire. I stopped by your house today, and nobody opened the door. I thought somebody got to you," Henry responded, his voice thick with concern.

"I am okay; I needed to talk to you immediately, so I set out to find you. I have so many things to tell you." Claire told him, her tone holding the urgency that she felt.

"What's going on?" Henry asked concern etched across his face.

Claire looked around before walking him toward her car. They both sat inside, and she made sure they were on a crowded street where nobody could attack them before taking a deep breath and turning to him.

"The past few days I have been looking deeper into what we found that day at the station. Remember the journal we found? I read it and I found several entries in it that prove that not only was my Grandfather discovered but he was also betrayed by someone close to him" she tells him and his eyes widen in shock.

"But who?" Henry whispered, and she shook her head as disappointed as him.

"I don't know. He didn't mention any names there, but he did say that he has started hiding clues for someone else to find so they can finish his job." Claire explains to him, sending him into deep thoughts.

"It makes sense; whatever we found could only be found if he wanted someone to find it. But how will we find out who that person is?" He wondered out loud.

"Today, I was at the cafe where you and I met for the first time. A man approached me, and he told me that he and my Grandfather were involved in this whole thing. He told me that whoever betrayed him was someone that I knew. He told me to be careful and to go back to where everything started." Claire filled him in,

Henry's eyes widened. *"Did he say who he was? What else did he tell you?"*

"No," Claire shook her head. *"He didn't give me his name, just that he was connected to everything—maybe even part of it. He hinted that there are people watching us, trying to keep the truth buried. He told me... he told me that the station is tied to something much bigger than we imagined, and we need to move fast before they come after us."*

Henry ran a hand through his hair, the gravity of the situation settling in. *"We need to act now. If what he says is true, we don't have much time."*

Claire nodded, her pulse quickening. *"He also gave me this,"* She told him as she handed him the small note he had left behind.

Henry took it from her hand carefully, opening it as he peered inside. Claire watched as his eyebrows furrowed with confusion, too. She had hoped that he would know what this meant, but it was clear that he didn't have any clue.

"These are coordinates, and I have no idea where they lead," Claire told him, a hint of disappointment in her voice.

"This is so much more complicated than I thought. We need to think about this. Do you remember your Grandfather being close with anybody?" Henry asked her, and Claire tried her best to remember.

"Grandpa talked to everyone kindly. I don't know who he was close with; he had so many friends. The only person that I ever saw him be very close with was my Uncle. He was the youngest son Grandpa had, and they used to be very close. But in his last few years, they became distant; I don't think he would know anything." Claire told him that she remembered the time when her Uncle and grandpa were always together.

She had no idea what caused them to fall out, but nobody in the family talked about it, and soon after, Claire moved out of the family house they once shared.

"Maybe these coordinates will lead us somewhere. I tried to contact your Grandfather's colleagues, but none of them answered. It's almost as if they are intentionally ignoring me. that was why I was unable to stop by the past few days." He explained and she nodded.

Everything was a mess and neither of them had an idea of what to do. Claire's mind raced as she tried to figure something out, but suddenly, she remembered the map that she had found in her Grandfather's stuff and all the places that he had marked.

"Henry... would you be able to find this place using the coordinates on the map that we found in Grandpa's stuff?" Claire asked, and Henry nodded.

Without wasting another second, they turned around and went back to where Claire had left the map. As soon as the map was in Henry's hand, he started concentrating, trying to find the answers while I stood there with bated breath.

Claire's heart pounded as she recalled the stranger's warning. She and Henry were getting closer to the truth, but that truth came with a price. The danger was real, and it was closing in on them.

Minutes ticked by in silence as Claire waited until Henry finally looked up.

"This doesn't make any sense." He said quietly and my heart suddenly started beating faster as went over to him and looked at the place that he had highlighted.

"That's my house..." Claire whispered, frozen to the spot at the new twist of events.

Chapter 7: The Final Puzzle

Claire and Henry were both unsure of what to make of their recent discovery. Claire grappled to make sense of what she was seeing. Maybe they were making a mistake; maybe this wasn't what these coordinates meant. But it seemed too weird to be a coincidence. What are the chances that the one hint that the man gave her led to her house?

"If you want to know more, you'll have to look at the place where it all began. Places that you are most comfortable in and that you know well hold the biggest clues."

Was it possible that her Grandfather had left clues back in the same house where he had last been? The thought that all of this led back to her family house sent a chill down her spine. Her thoughts tangled in a web of confusion, disbelief, and a growing sense of dread. How could this all come back to the one place she thought she knew so well?

'Claire?" Henry called out her name, pulling her out of her thoughts.

She instantly pulled herself out of her head and turned to Henry, who looked just as confused and troubled as she felt.

"It's weird that this leads back to my family house. Could we be reading this wrong, Henry?" she asked him, unable to process her thoughts. Her gut was silent, unable to lead her to the right path.

"I don't know, but it doesn't feel like it was a mistake. There seems to be some connection between your house and this whole mess. Your Grandfather highlighted it too for a reason." He pointed out.

"Do you think he kept the real proof in the house?" Claire asked, and Henry shrugged.

"That could happen. Who is still living in the house?" Henry questioned.

"My parents still live there, but they have been traveling almost continuously for the past few years. They are still not here. Other than them, one of my aunts and uncle live there." She told him, and his eyebrows raised in question.

"Are they both there alone?" Henry interrogated, and she nodded.

"My aunt Teresa, my father's sister, was recently divorced so she has been staying in the family house since then. And my Uncle Albert, my father's cousin's brother, is also there." she shared with him.

Henry's eyebrows shot up at that.

"Albert is there?" He questioned, surprise evident in his voice.

"You know Uncle Albert?" She shot back, surprised at the familiarity in his voice.

"Of course. He was always in and out of the station. Your Grandfather and him were pretty close. Ever since his father's death, your Grandfather took him under his wing. But the last time I saw him, he was planning to leave the country. I thought he did." Claire's eyes widened at this new information.

She was too young to remember everything, but she knew that Uncle Albert lived with them because his parents died. However, she had no idea that her Grandfather and he had been that close. Neither had she ever heard any talk of him going aboard.

"I had no idea about that. But then again, he and I have never been that close." Claire shared with Henry, who nodded understandingly.

Uncle Albert had always been distant, even when she was a child, and she rarely saw him after she moved out. The last time she had seen him was at her Grandfather's funeral, where he had been strangely quiet, almost detached.

Something about him had always made her uneasy, but she had never paid it much attention—until now.

"We should go to your house," Henry told her softly, and she took a moment before nodding.

She didn't even know if she was ready for what she was about to find out. She hadn't gone back to that house in a long time, simply because it reminded her too much of her Grandfather, and thinking about him made the pain of losing him even worse. But she had to face it, go back there to finally uncover the truth and put an end to this whole thing.

"Yes," she agreed, though her voice wavered. The house felt like a looming specter, holding secrets she wasn't sure she was ready to uncover.

The ride to the house was quiet, the weight of the unknown pressing down on both of them. The familiar streets passed by in a blur as Claire tried to make sense of everything. Her Grandfather's death, the strange man at the café, the coordinates, the betrayal—all of it pointed to something far more sinister than she had ever imagined.

The house wasn't far from the station, but soon, they were there. Claire took one last deep breath before she got out of the car, ready to face the awaiting truth that would change her life forever.

Henry looked at her once, his presence comforting.

"Don't worry, I am here." He told her reassuringly and she tried to give him a smile but failed. Her nerves were barely letting her move anyway.

They moved closer to the house, and Claire couldn't help but notice that nothing about the house had changed. It was the same as it had always been. But now, it seemed almost menacing, as if it were hiding something dark within its walls.

Thankfully, she still had the key to the house in her keychain. She had never bothered to remove it, even though she doubted she would ever come back to this place once she moved out.

She saw a car in the driveway and wondered who was home, her aunt or uncle. It had been years since she had seen either of them and didn't know what to expect. She opened the door as quietly as possible. Henry and she had both agreed to get in and out of the house as silently as possible. It was a big house, almost a mansion, and with only two people living in it, they could easily get in without anyone noticing.

Claire led Henry up the stairs where her Grandfather's room had been. All the while, she looked around, remembering how she once used to live there. The house held so many memories of Claire's childhood. This was the reason why Claire had avoided coming to this house since her Grandfather had passed. She couldn't bear to be here knowing that her Grandfather was no longer with her.

It was here that he had spent the most time with her. He had taught her how to play almost every game, how to ride a bicycle, and how to spell out her own name. Claire had grown up with her Grandfather by her side all her life, and being in the house made her realize just how hollow her life had become ever since he had passed away.

As soon as she opened the door to her Grandfather's room, she was greeted by a storm of dust and darkness. It was clear that nobody had entered this room or bothered to keep it clean since her Grandfather died. Henry coughed a little as he batted away the dust and tried to find the switchboard. Fortunately, he found it and turned the light on flooding the room with light.

Nostalgia hit Claire so hard, tears welled in her eyes.

This room had been her safe haven, a place where she found comfort and safety in all cases. Whenever she was sad, mad, or her parents were mad at her, she would run here, knowing that her Grandfather would always be there for her. He would always make it better for her. The quietness in the room taunted her, reminding Claire of her loss. Her life was as empty as this room ever since she had lost him, and this quest had made her miss him more than ever.

She didn't know when tears leaked from her eyes, only that Henry was wrapping his arms around her in a fatherly hug as she comforted her. She had tried so hard to stay strong this whole time, but being here, in this room, was enough to make her give in. She had avoided this place for years because she knew she wouldn't be able to keep herself together if she returned to his room again.

Henry led her to her Grandfather's bed and made her sit down, trying to help her calm down. It took her a few minutes to compose herself before she could finally wipe her tears away.

"I am sorry," she apologized to Henry, feeling embarrassed for breaking down like that in front of him.

"You have no reason to apologize, Claire. You have been so strong this whole time. I know how close you were with your Grandfather. It must be really difficult for you to do this, but you have come this far. Don't give in just yet. Finish what you started; only you can do what your Grandfather couldn't." he told her softly, trying to motivate her.

Claire nodded, knowing he was right. She was doing this for her Grandfather, and he had never taught her to give up. Pulling herself together once and for all, she finally stood up.

"Let's put an end to this." She told Henry and he smiled at her proudly as he nodded.

They started searching the room, hoping to find something that would help them. They moved methodically through the room, checking every nook, every corner, but finding nothing out of the ordinary. Claire's frustration grew with each passing minute, her fear that they were missing something important gnawing at her.

Soon, they had searched the room thrice and found nothing, leading to a sense of frustration and helplessness.

"There is nothing here. What are we missing, Henry?" she said as she turned toward Henry who looked just as confused as her.

"Is there any other place your Grandfather spent a lot of time in? any place other than his room that we could look in?" Henry tried to come up with something, but Claire shook her head.

The only place her Grandfather was ever found was either his room or her room.

"He was always in his own room or in mine when he was spending time with me. Otherwise, he would spend his time out of the house." She admitted to him.

"Then let's go check out your room," Henry suggested, and Claire's eyebrows furrowed.

"My room? But why would he hide something in my room?" she asked hesitantly. She didn't see why he would hide such important clues in her room.

"You said it yourself that he spent the most time in your room other than his room. It would make sense, anyway. If the betrayer knew that your Grandfather knew the truth, he would have tried to look in his room to get rid of the evidence. Your Grandfather was a smart man, Claire. Nobody would look in your room; maybe that's why he didn't hide anything here." Henry explained to her, and Claire's mouth opened at his words.

Although it seemed a little far-fetched, it also sounded like something that her Grandfather would do. Her heart raced at the thought as she nodded, and they both rushed out of his room and toward her room.

Her room was almost next to her Grandfather's, but it was in a turning corner and was often missed by people. She thought of how if somebody did come looking for evidence, they might just have missed that there was a room there at all. If her Grandfather had indeed left the evidence in her room, she wouldn't be surprised. He had always been a clever man.

As soon as they entered her room, Claire's heart ached as she saw everything that she had kept there exactly as she left it. But she held herself together, reminding herself that she did not have the time to break down. They instantly got to searching the room, trying to find something that could be evidence.

They searched intensely for a few minutes but found nothing. Claire was almost about to give up when her attention went to the bookshelf in her room. Something in her made her push the bookshelf away, and when she looked behind, she gasped, gaining Henry's attention.

There was a door behind the bookshelf that Claire had never seen before. She had spent her entire life here, but she had never known it existed. She exchanged a look with Henry, both of them knowing that they had finally found what they were looking for.

Chapter 8: Confrontation

The secret room in front of Claire and Henry was nothing less of a paradox box. Mysterious, unpredictable, and seemingly dangerous. They knew that this room in front of them held all the secrets and probably the final evidence that they needed to find to end this whole thing once and for all. But whatever awaited them in that room made them pause, unable to move.

Claire was going through a myriad of emotions. There was so much that was going on inside her that she didn't even know how to react. It blew her away that not only did her Grandfather hide whatever evidence he had in *her* room but also that this hidden door had been in her room forever, and she had never even known.

Henry and Claire shared a look, one that spoke volumes. This was it, the final step before they would finally get to the end of this whole quest. With a nod, they both decided to take a step toward the room, ready to face the truth that awaited them. Henry was the one who pushed the door open, the sound of creaking filled the silent space between them.

Claire held her breath as she peeked inside only to find a dark spiral staircase leading down into the unknown. Her heart was racing from anticipation and nervousness, the sound of her own breathing loud in her ears. She had no idea what she was going to find down there but she was ready to find out.

It was clear that nobody had been in this room for years from the way the air inside the room was stale as if it hadn't been disturbed in years. Dust particles floated lazily in the narrow beam of light that filtered through the room.

Henry stood beside her, his face set in grim determination. They didn't say anything to each other, the silence between them filled with suspense and they pulled out their phones, turned on the flashlights, and started to descend the staircase.

The staircase went on forever until they finally found the end of it and found themselves in a dimly lit room. They stepped inside cautiously, the weight of the moment pressing down on them.

The room was sparse, with only a small table, a few shelves, and an old wooden chest pushed against one wall. Claire and Henry looked around, scanning the room. They were unsure of what to do and where to look first.

Claire walked toward the table first, taking cautious steps toward it. She was scared that if she took one wrong step she could end up messing something up. Her eyes fell on the chest that sat on the desk and she made a beeline for it.

A strange sense of foreboding washed over her. She felt a shiver run down her spine as she approached it, her hands trembling slightly as she reached for the latch.

"What do you think is in there?" Henry's voice was low, almost a whisper as if he was afraid to disturb whatever lay inside.

Claire hesitated for a moment before answering. *"I don't know,"*

The air around them was tense as if a clock was ticking and someone was breathing down Claire's neck as she finally started to open the chest.

She expected to find it full, filled with evidence and proof that would finally reveal the answer to this mystery, but instead, she found it mostly empty, except for a lone key sitting at the bottom of the chest.

Claire blinked, confused at what she was seeing. She slowly reached for the key and pulled it out to show Henry.

"A key?" he asked out loud, just as confused as she was.

"What do you think this key is for? What does it lead to?" Claire asked him as she inspected the key. She had no idea where it led to or what it opened.

Henry looked just as blank as her mind was right now. Once again, they found themselves at a dead-end. They had no idea what to make of this new clue.

They both felt like they were once again at square one. Claire closed her eyes briefly, trying to think what this key could mean. Her Grandfather had hidden it in her room for a reason; all she needed to do now was figure out what that reason was.

"It doesn't make sense for him to have a secret room like this where he would only hide a key. Whatever he has hidden has to be in here." Henry said to Claire, who was lost in thoughts.

"Maybe he didn't want the information to get into the wrong hands. This room could be easily discovered. We are missing something here." Claire responded as she turned and decided to look closely at the room they were in.

It was dark there, the only light filling the space was from their phone. Claire used her flashlight to inspect the room. She moved toward the shelf on the nearby wall, looking at the few books in there.

She wondered why they were there in the first place as she started to pull each one out. She didn't recognize any of the books on the shelf, another thing that was odd for Claire.

Her Grandfather had always kept her involved in whatever book he was reading, but if he owned these books, she had never seen them before. She decided to skim through one, flipping pages distractedly, when suddenly she noticed red markings inside the books.

She noticed how the word 'behind' had been highlighted in the book twice or thrice while the rest of the book remained unmarked. She instantly perked up at the discovery.

"Henry!" Claire exclaimed, her voice filled with an urgency that had Henry rushing to her.

"What did you find?" he asked her just as she reached her side and she showed him the markings on the book.

Wordlessly, they both started inspecting the other books and trying to find other clues. Some of the books remained empty, but they found two other books that highlighted the same word over and over again. It took them only a minute to put the words together.

"Behind The Shelf"

Their eyes widened as they realized the message, and without wasting a minute, Henry started to move the shelf. Claire could feel her heart racing as they both worked to remove the shelf, only for it to reveal another door, this time locked.

Claire and Henry shared one last look before she inserted the key and unlocked the door. They both opened it, only to reveal a room that was a mess. There were papers everywhere as if somebody had gotten into a fight. Claire wondered what had happened there.

"Whatever Grandpa wanted me to find, it's here. I know it is." Claire said out loud, her voice echoing in the small room.

"Let's search," Henry said somberly as he moved toward the papers.

Claire followed his lead, grabbing one of the newspapers that had fallen on the floor. She read through it, noticing many interviews of powerful people that were all marked.

They continued to look, finding several marked newspapers highlighting matters of drug lords, human trafficking, and other heinous crimes. She neared the corner of the room, where she noticed something black lying on the ground.

Carefully, she picked it up only to realize that it was a voice recorder. Her senses heightened, knowing that a voice recording would be the most crucial of evidence in a case like that.

She pressed play, putting the object near her ear, hoping it was still working. The recorder crackled to life, and the sound of Claire's Grandfather's voice filled the room, making her heart ache with longing.

"Albert, I know what you've done. You can't keep this hidden forever."

The voice of her Grandfather was strained and weary but filled with a determination that sent chills down Claire's spine. She could hear the tremor in his voice, the fear he must have felt.

Another voice followed, cold and familiar. *"You don't understand, old man. I did what had to be done. You were always too weak to see the bigger picture."*

Claire's breath caught in her throat as she recognized the voice of Uncle Albert. The calmness in his tone was chilling, devoid of any remorse.

"You betrayed me, Albert. You betrayed the family," her Grandfather's voice responded, filled with sorrow and disbelief.

"It wasn't about the family," Albert spat. *"It was about survival. You and your righteousness would have brought us all down. I had to make a choice, and I chose to protect myself. I did what was necessary."*

"So you choose to use my trust as a way to make black money? I trusted you with everything, took you in, and you used my station to expand your horrible criminal business?" Anger surged in her Grandfather's voice.

"You only took me in because you felt guilty. You weren't there for my parents when they needed you the most, old man. You weren't there for your own son because your ego stopped you." Albert's voice raised in anger.

"Your father was an addict, and so was your mom! What did you expect me to do?" There was undeniable anger in her Grandfather's voice, but there was also an undercurrent of pain. It was clear that whatever happened between his son and him brought him no joy.

"I was a child. Nobody bothered to think of me, so now I don't care about you. I am warning you, stay out of this, or you won't like the consequences." Albert threatened in a chilling tone that made Claire's breath hitch.

Claire felt sick to her stomach, her hands trembling as she listened to the vile words. Her eyes filled with tears, but she forced herself to listen to the end, even as her heart broke.

"Are you threatening me, boy?" Her Grandfather asked, his voice low, disbelieving.

"Take it as you want, old man. But if you come in my way, I will not hesitate to get rid of you." He said, not even hesitating.

It was then that the voice recording ended, leaving Henry and Claire standing there in shock. They couldn't come to terms with what they had just heard.

The air around them was heavy with silence, a looming feeling of dread surrounding them. Claire felt weak in her knees and wanted to sink down and mourn her Grandfather all over again.

The man she had known as her uncle, the man who had lived under the same roof as her, had been the one responsible for her Grandfather's death.

Henry's face was pale from shock, too, but he was the one who found his voice first. *"Claire, we need to take this to the authorities. There are a lot of things I found, too. There are photographs of Albert in meetings and all the records of where he has been, as well as the secret meetings where money was exchanged. Your Grandfather has kept track of everything. We finally have everything we need to get him arrested."* He told her, but Claire couldn't process it yet. The weight of the evidence was too overwhelming.

"I can't believe the man who shared a roof with us for so long is the one who killed my Grandfather," Claire whispered, her voice trembling.

"I know. Your Grandfather must have been crushed. But Claire, we need to get out of here. Let's finally rest this case once and for all." Henry urged Claire, concerned.

Claire nodded slowly, wiping her tears as she pulled herself together. Her sadness was heavy but not more than her anger. She was burning with the fire to make her uncle pay for what he had done.

Both Henry and her left the room and made their way back to her room. They rushed to push the shelf back in place when they heard a creak behind them.

Claire's head whipped back only to find her Uncle Albert standing there. She gulped at the sight of him, her blood running cold. His eyes were dark, filled with an intensity that made Claire's blood run cold. The look on his face was one of pure malice.

Albert stepped into the room, his gaze fixed on the voice recorder in Henry's hand. *"I see you found it,"* he said, his voice deceptively calm. *"I was hoping you wouldn't, but it seems your grandfather's cunning runs in the family."*

Anger rose inside Claire at his words. *"How dare you stand there and say that? You killed him, betrayed the man who gave you a life. How can you stand yourself? How do you live with yourself, Uncle Albert?"* Claire spit out the word Uncle, disgusted that she had never considered him family.

Albert's lips twisted into a cruel smile. *"I did what I had to do, Claire. You wouldn't understand, just like your Grandfather didn't."*

"Walk out of the way; we are done here," Claire warned him, hoping to make it out of there.

"I am afraid I can't do that. I didn't want to do this, Claire. I told your Grandfather to stay out of my business, too, but he didn't listen. Look where that got him. Now, you seem to have made the same mistake." Albert shook his head as if disappointed, but the threat in his voice was clear.

"You don't scare me, Albert. Your game is over." Claire said just as she noticed movement behind his shoulder but forced herself to stay indifferent.

Albert's smile faded, his eyes narrowing dangerously. *"You think this is over? You're more naïve than I thought."*

Both Henry and Claire watched as if in slow motion as his hand reached toward his pocket, realizing what was about to happen. But before he could point the handgun at them, another figure came up behind him and slammed what looked like a vase on his head, making him lose his grip on the gun as he groaned from pain.

"Aunt Teresa!" Claire exclaimed as Albert fell to the ground, unconscious.

Claire's aunt's face was red, her breathing heavy as she stared at Albert.

Henry rushed to Albert, checking his pulse quickly before taking a sigh of relief.

"He is out cold." He announced but no one responded, the weight of everything that had just happened settling in.

"He killed my father," Aunt Teresa finally spoke, her voice more broken than Claire had ever heard.

Tears welled in her eyes as she walked toward her, pulling her into a hug as her eyes met Henry's.

"It's okay, it's over." She said, more to herself as she finally let out a breath she didn't know she was holding.

She had finally done it.

Chapter 9: Justice Served

The next few hours were a blur of actions. Claire didn't have any idea when Henry left the room to call the authorities, only that soon the sound of sirens filled the silence, and the house that had been silent and empty suddenly became the center of everyone's attention. The authorities cast a look of pity toward her, most of them knowing her as they took Uncle Albert away.

Claire, on the other hand, felt numb. She should be feeling victorious, overfilled with joy for finally exposing the truth and bringing her grandfather justice. But she didn't feel anything in that moment, only shock and grief. The man who was responsible for killing her Grandfather was someone with whom she had shared a roof. All this time that she had been grieving her Grandfather, he had been right there, and she hadn't even known.

She had no idea how to deal with the aftermath of everything and no one to go to. She sat there in her old room, the same room that she hadn't visited in years now, because the memories she had there haunted her. The irony of the situation wasn't lost on her. She had tried so hard to avoid this house, this room, just to avoid having to face the hurricane of emotions she had buried inside ever since her Grandfather had passed away.

Sitting in her room alone, her tears flowed freely. She didn't know why she was crying; only that her tears flowed uncontrollably. She realized just how much she had buried deep into her heart. When she got the news of her Grandfather's death, she remembered staying in the stage of denial, not able to come to terms with the loss of somebody who had been there for her at every stage of her life.

As a result, she had never truly dealt with his death properly. Instead, she shoved all her feelings in one corner and decided to move on without ever facing the grief that she had buried deep in her heart.

But when she returned to the station, ready to bring him justice, everything that she had long buried was starting to simmer all over again. And now that everything is done and the culprit behind this whole thing is caught, Claire has to deal with the full intensity of all the emotions she had spent so long trying to run from.

So many years had passed, and she still couldn't go a day without missing her Grandfather. The man had risked his own life just to be able to expose the wrongdoings of someone whom he considered family. As if losing him already wasn't bad enough, the realization that he died at the hands of someone they all trusted made it even more hurtful.

The only thing that made any of this better was that Claire and Henry were able to expose the truth and finish what her Grandfather started. She didn't even want to think of how he must have felt in his final moments when he was left to wonder if his life had been worth sacrificing for something he couldn't even finish.

A soft knock sounded from the door, and Claire looked up to find her parents standing there. They had both taken a short drive to the neighboring town and had raced back when they heard the news.

Wiping her tears away, Claire looked up at them. They both looked like they, too, had cried.

"Can we come in?" Her mother asked softly, and she nodded.

They both sat down on either side of her, staying silent.

"How did you find out?" Her father was the one who broke the silence.

"He left clues right here in my room. He spent so much time trying to collect evidence to expose him, but he was too late." Her voice came out hoarse as she told him.

"He knew that Albert was responsible?" Claire's mother asked, her tone disbelieving.

"He knew everything. Uncle Albert threatened him to stay away and not expose him, but Grandpa went ahead and did it anyway. And that is what cost him." Claire could barely keep herself together.

It was depressing to sit there and talk about her Grandfather and discuss how he died. But it was the closure that Claire's family had been deprived of.

"He would have been proud of you, you know?" Claire's mother said after a pause, turning to look at her.

Claire's heart filled up with sadness at her words. She didn't want people to tell her that he would have been proud; she wanted him to be here, hug her, and tell her how proud she had made him. But it was too late for that now.

"It's been years since he passed away. I am too late." She admitted the thought that had been killing her from within.

Both her parents turned toward her, sharing a look of pity and heartbreak. They both knew just how attached their daughter had been to her Grandfather. When he died, they didn't know how to break the news to her or help her later. When she shut down, they both felt helpless, for it was always her Grandfather who had been there for her in difficult times. Both her parents were lost.

But now, as they sat there and saw just how much of a mess their daughter was, they couldn't help but feel guilty for not being there for her sooner.

"You are not late, sweetie. If it hadn't been for you, we might never have found out the truth, and Albert would have gone unpunished. You outdid yourself, and your grandpa would be very, very proud of you." Her mother told her.

"Your Grandfather always knew that you would do things no one could, and you did just that. You might have gotten here a little late, but I know that he is up there somewhere, smiling at you proudly. If he was here, he would tell me how right he was. He always told me you would make me proud one day, and you did just that, Claire. Never doubt that. Your Grandfather might not be here in person today, but he is alive in our hearts." His father continued, his own eyes filling up with tears.

Claire looked up at them, feeling better about herself.

"And if you still doubt us, just know that your Grandfather never needed you to solve this case to be proud of you. He was always proud of you, and that doesn't change because he isn't here anymore." Her father told her softly, and Claire felt overwhelmed by emotions at his words.

She hugged her father, letting herself cry into his arms for the first time ever since the first time he told her about her Grandfather's death. That night, Claire and her family sat together, reminiscing about the time they spent with her Grandfather, finally getting the closure that they needed to say goodbye.

In the next few days, the news of what had happened spread like wildfire. The arrest of Albert had come as a shock to everyone, spreading confusion amongst the neighbors. The small community of people that had been close to Claire's family was appalled as they heard the truth of what had happened to her Grandfather.

Claire's Grandfather had been a man respected by many, and all those people had been heartbroken at the news of his death. But now that they knew the truth, the air was buzzing with whispers and murmurs as they all talked together, unable to comprehend what had happened.

The trial for Albert had been set after two days of arrest, and on the day of the trial, the entire community was gathered outside the courthouse, wanting to know the final decision. The number of people who were livid on behalf of Claire's Grandfather made her realize how much influence he had had in their society, and that only made it sadder.

The day of the trial was a particularly difficult one for Claire. Standing at the edge of where the crowd was gathered, Claire felt a myriad of emotions that were too intense for her to process all at once. She was going through a whirlwind of relief and sorrow that dragged her down, but she also felt peaceful that she had finally done what her Grandfather had set out to do.

Henry stood beside her, just like he had since the very beginning. They both had gone through so much together and as they stood there together, looking at all the people who looked betrayed and mad at the same time. Soon enough, Albert was led out his hands cuffed as he was pushed forward.

Claire had always seen the man as a proud and imposing figure. Even in those last moments when he was threatening her he felt impossible to defeat. But the man who was being led into the courthouse was nothing more than a man broken by his own sins. The crowd outside went wild, shouting angrily, a collective voice of the town finally seeing the truth that had been hidden for so long.

"Let's go," Henry said, pulling her out of her thoughts.

Claire turned to him, unable to move in the direction of the courthouse. She didn't know how to do this, how to stand there in front of the man who killed her Grandfather.

"I don't know if I can do this, Henry." She murmured, her throat dry.

"You can, you have come so far, Claire. You can take the final step now. Finish what you set out to finish and put an end to this." He told her motivationally.

His words hit the mark. Claire knew he was right; she had come all this way, and if she quit right now, she wouldn't be able to face herself. So, with a deep breath, she took a steady step toward the courthouse, ready to face the man who had ruined everything.

The trial was swift, and the evidence Claire and Henry had uncovered left no room for doubt. The voice recordings, photographs, and documents detailing Albert's corruption and betrayal were presented in court, painting a damning picture of a man who had sacrificed his own family for power and greed. Along with all the other powerful and influential people who were just as involved in this dark business as Albert was. Her

Grandfather had made sure to collect enough evidence to ensure that each and every person involved could be proven guilty and charged for their crimes. The jury's verdict was unanimous—guilty on all charges.

Henry and Claire left the courthouse together, watching as the man responsible for so much devastation was dragged away. Claire felt at peace as if a huge responsibility had been taken down from her shoulders. She thought of everything that had happened in the past few weeks as she investigated and how much people around her had helped her.

She had started this journey thinking that she would have to find out the truth on her own, but if it hadn't been for Henry and the mystery man at the café, she wouldn't have been able to get to the bottom of this case and disclose the truth. She turned toward Henry, her eyes filled with appreciation and gratefulness as he looked at her.

"Thank you. For everything." She told him gratefully.

"You don't need to thank me, Claire. You did the most of everything; you found the strength and bravery to risk your life and do what is right. I am only glad that I could be there for you and help you." He told her, smiling at him softly.

"You did more than help me, Henry. If it hadn't been for you, I would have never been able to do this." She said, and he smiled.

They both stood outside the courthouse in a peaceful silence, finally able to be at peace now that they had found the closure that they were finding. Claire let out a deep breath, letting this dark chapter of her life finally come to an end and heal from the weight of her family's past.

Chapter 10: A New Dawn

The morning light filtered into the station as Claire entered it. It was empty, like the day she stepped into it for the first time ever since her Grandfather died. But now, instead of an abandoned crumbling structure, isolated and left to its bitter fate, Claire now stood in a newly renovated station with polished floors and the scent of fresh paint in the air.

Looking at how much the station had changed, she couldn't help but feel pleased and a little proud of herself. After the case had been put to rest, Claire didn't immediately return here, needing some time to herself to come to terms with her feelings and make peace with everything that had happened. But the minute she was ready, the station was the first place she visited.

This station was where her Grandfather had spent most of his life. She had as many memories here as she did in her house. Her Grandfather's hard work and goodwill had made the station the best around there, and with him gone, the station, too, went through a downfall, and nobody ever bothered to change that.

But Claire knew that she wanted to change that. It was depressing to look at a place where she had spent her happiest moments in look like that. She wanted the place that her Grandfather had spent so much time and energy on to still be thriving. She knew it was no easy job. It was going to take time and energy to return to what it used to be like, but she was willing to do it. Nothing mattered to her more than doing what she knew her Grandfather would have done if he was alive.

Claire walked around the station, taking it all in. Even though the station had undergone a major transformation, Claire had ensured that some things remained the same. One of which was her Grandfather's room. She remembered how he paid attention to every intricate detail as he set his room, and she didn't want to change anything about it. Other than getting that room cleaned and repainted, she left it untouched.

But the rest of the station was unrecognizable. Claire had paid attention to every detail, spending most of her time in the station as she overlooked the process herself. What was once a dark and decaying space was now bright and welcoming once again, just like how she remembered it to be when she was young.

When she had announced her plans to bring the station back to life she hadn't expected her family and everyone else in the society to support her so much. But seeing how quickly the station had been renovated and was ready to run again showed the enthusiasm most people had as they helped her in every way possible in rebuilding this place.

She remembered that her Grandfather had dreamed of making this station one of the biggest and most successful stations. He was always working hard, putting in so much effort to ensure that it lived up to its potential. In the time that he had been alive the station was the best, a testament to his hard work and drive toward making it the best that this place had to offer.

As she toured the place, she came upon the section where she had decorated herself to honor her Grandfather. She wanted him to get the recognition and praise that he deserved, not only for all the years that he had spent in this station and working hard for it to become the best but also for sacrificing his life just to save the reputation and honor of this place.

There was large picture that she had hung on that wall along with all the other achievements he had had over the years. It made her feel better to know that he would always be remembered by people who visited this station. It didn't matter that she was the one who was bringing this station back to life; it would always be her Grandfather who truly did anything for this station.

But despite that, she was proud of herself for all that she had come. In the pursuit of justice, there were times when she doubted herself. She had put her life in jeopardy just to ensure that the truth would come out, but even then, she wasn't truly sure if she would be successful in the end. But now, as she stood here, she had to admit that she did it.

The sound of footsteps approached her, and she turned around to see who it was, only to find Henry coming her way. She noticed the way Henry took in the place and the way his eyes shined with nostalgia that she was sure he felt.

He too had spent a lot of time in this station, she remembered, and seeing it come back to life must have been a important moment for him too.

“This place is unrecognizable,” he murmured as he came to a stop beside her before his eyes landed on her Grandfather’s picture.

“I know; I wanted it to look alive again,” Claire told him softly, standing there with him in comfortable silence.

“You have outdone yourself, Claire. I hope you know that.” Henry said after a few minutes, turning toward her, his voice full of emotions.

“I hope so. It was his dream that this station thrives and becomes the very best.” She told him, and he nodded.

“So what now?” Henry asked after a short pause, and Claire turned to him in confusion.

“What do you mean?” she asked.

“I mean, what’s the next step? Now that you are done with this case, what are you planning to do next?” he questioned, looking at her with curiosity.

His question caught her off-guard, making her question herself. For so long, this case had consumed her. She had spent every living, breathing moment of her time trying to figure out the truth and reveal it to the world. But now that this case was closed, she had no idea what to do anymore.

"I... I haven't thought of it," she murmured, feeling lost all of a sudden.

Henry's expression softened at the expression on her face. "You've been through so much, Claire. It's okay to take a moment for yourself to figure out what you really want. You don't have to decide everything today."

Claire nodded, appreciating his words. He was right, of course. For the first time in what felt like years, she had the luxury of time—time to think, time to breathe, time to heal.

She could take some time off, spend some time to regroup, and truly get herself together before she went back to making her career.

Solving this case was a major success for her and her profile as an agent. She knew that getting a job would be no trouble now that she was free again, but she just didn't feel ready anymore.

Henry looked at her, feeling both pride and concern for her at the same time. If there was anyone who knew just how much she had gone through in this entire journey, it was him.

He had been there with her through every step of the way as they uncovered every new detail of this case and he was glad to see that she was doing all of this.

But at the same time, he couldn't help but feel troubled at the way she was struggling to move on. He knew how attached she had been to her Grandfather, but it was time for her to move on.

But pushing her didn't feel right, so instead, he left the topic alone. He stayed there with her for another few minutes, making small talk but mostly just offering her company so she wouldn't be alone.

They sat in her Grandfather's room, reminiscing about old memories they had in the station, exchanging stories with each other until Henry finally decided to leave.

"I'll see you tomorrow at the opening of the station, then," Henry told her as he started to depart, and she nodded quietly.

She suddenly looked sad, and Henry wanted to stay and make it better, but he decided to give her some space. She was still processing everything.

With that thought in mind, he turned around and left the room. He walked away from the station quietly. As he walked toward the exit, he couldn't help but feel weird, as if there was something he was missing.

But Henry pushed the feeling away, thinking of it as nothing more than paranoia. He left the station, but after walking for about ten minutes, he searched his pockets for his phone only to find it empty.

He paused, looking thoroughly just as he remembered that he had left his phone at the station. He considered walking away and getting it tomorrow but decided to turn around and get it then only.

As he walked back to the station there was something that was bothering but he just couldn't put a finger on it. As he entered the station the unsettling feeling followed him as his footsteps echoed in the silence.

"Claire?" He called out, having seen her car still outside, but no one responded.

Suddenly, a chill went down his spine as paranoia overtook him, and he rushed inside, trying to find her. He kept calling out her name, but no response came until he saw a figure on the floor, and his heart started to pound as he walked closer.

His heart sank as he came closer and found Claire lying on the floor, her body crumpled and surrounded by blood. His hands were trembling as he looked at the gruesome sight in front of him.

Henry froze, unable to process what he was seeing. This couldn't be real. It had to be some terrible mistake. He knelt down and reached out to touch her face. Her skin was cold, her lips pale. There was no warmth, no breath.

Despair filled him as he looked at her, wishing this was just a nightmare. He held her in his arms, the reality of her death sinking in as he looked at her.

After everything they had been through—after all the danger, the betrayal, the fight for justice—she was gone.

But the question that haunted him was what had happened in the past ten minutes?

But no one knew, and just like there were two bodies found in the same station, like a curse nobody could fight off.

Made in the USA
Columbia, SC
08 April 2025

05e1afb0-fb87-4347-aced-2d9a2a3240abR01